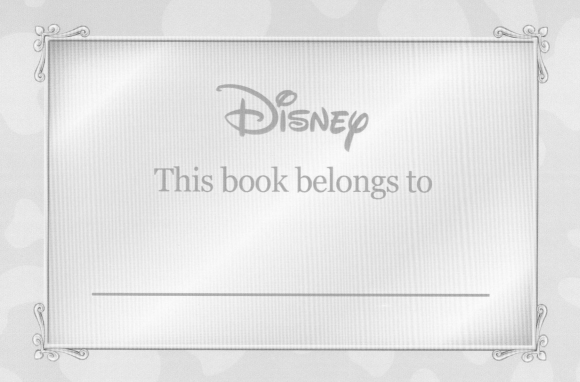

Disney

This book belongs to

_____

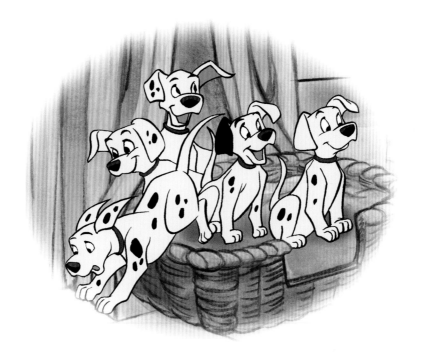

Written by K.R. Knight

101 DALMATIANS

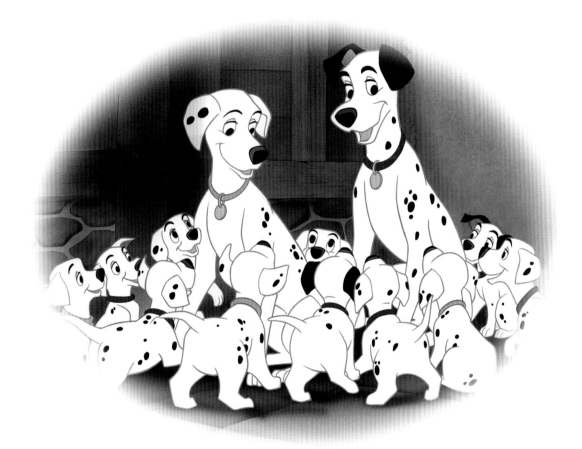

Puppy Parade

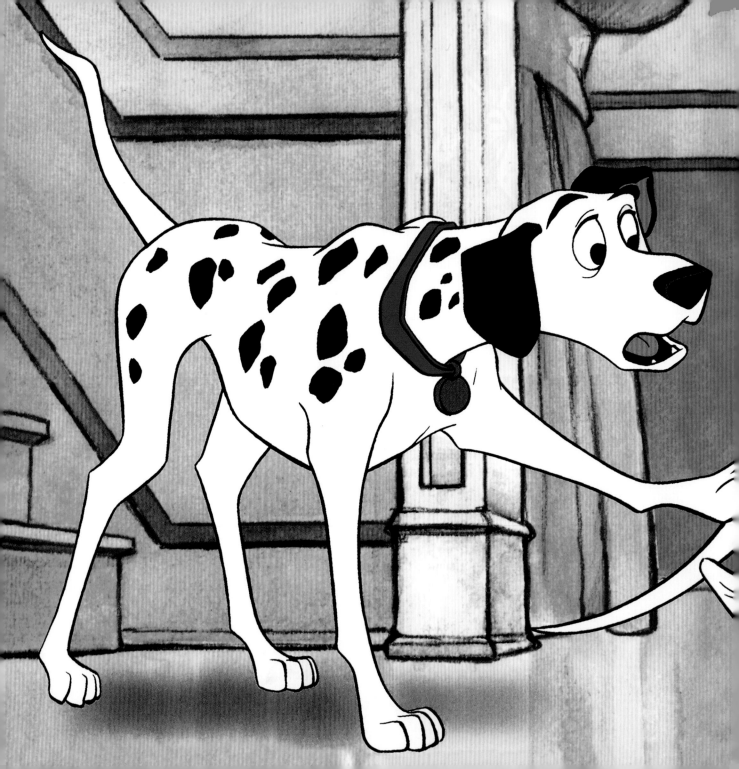

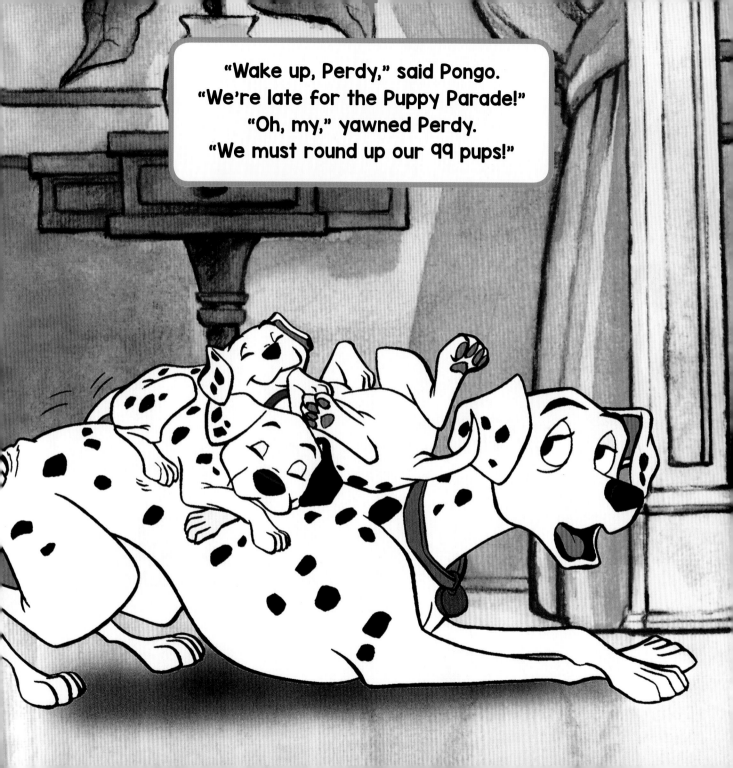

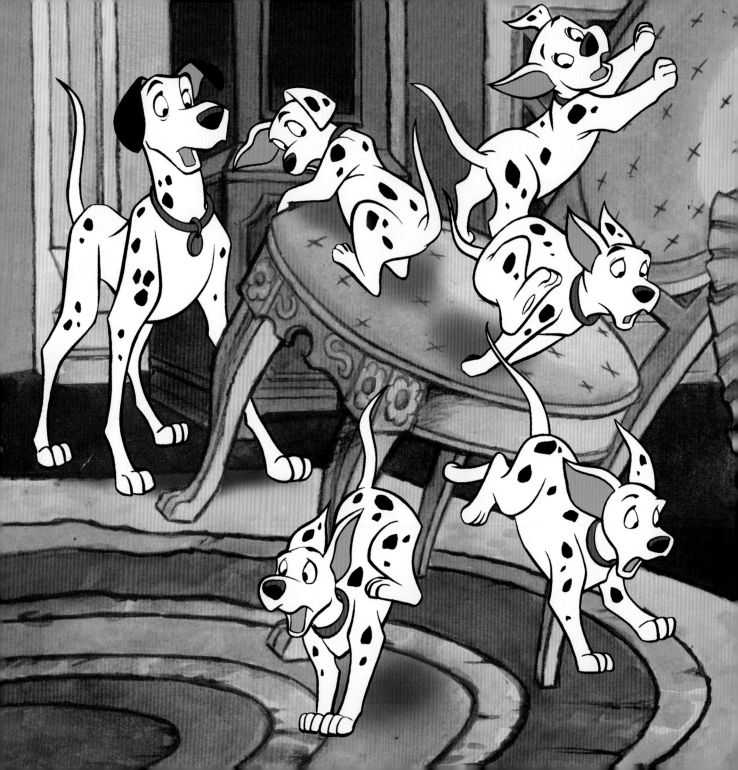

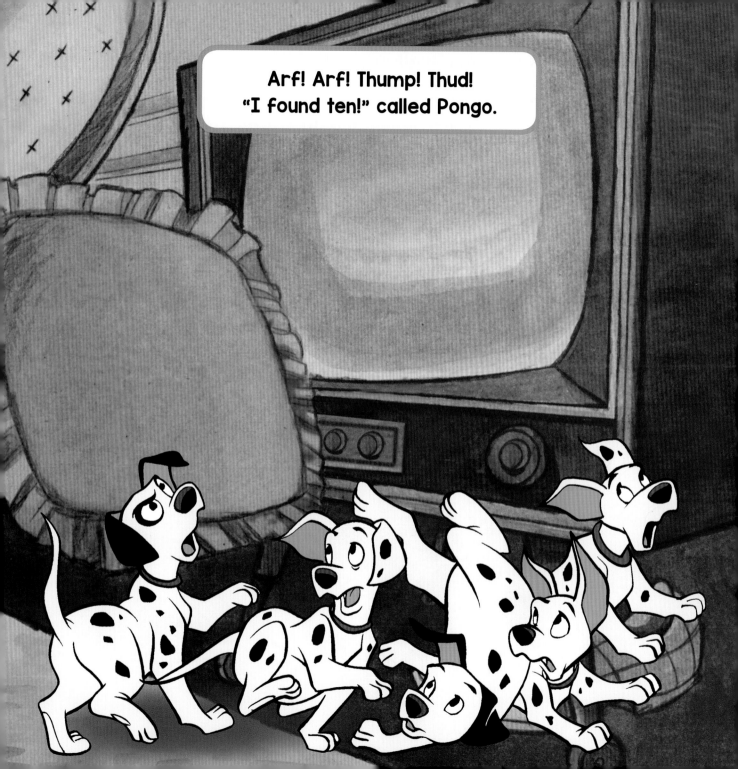

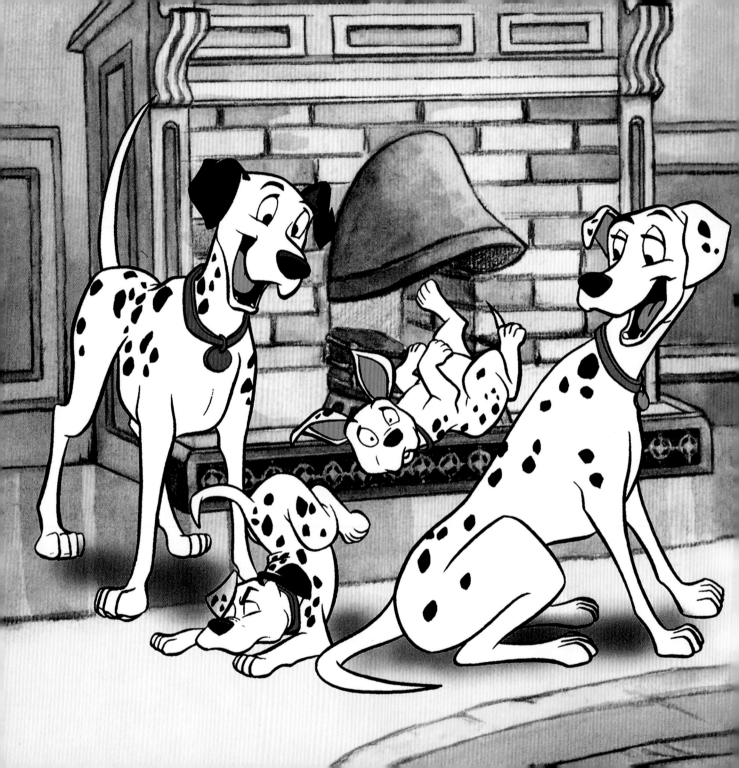

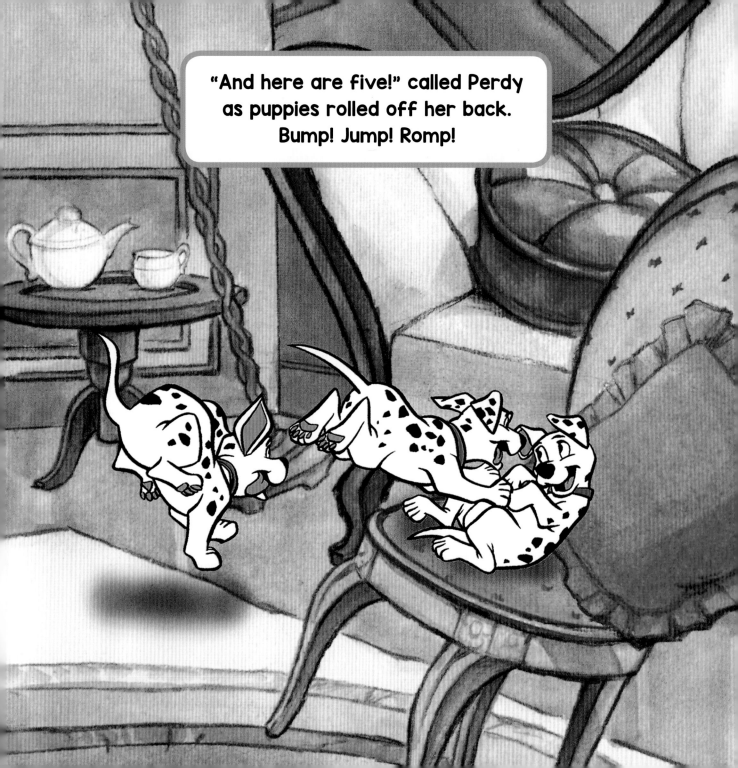

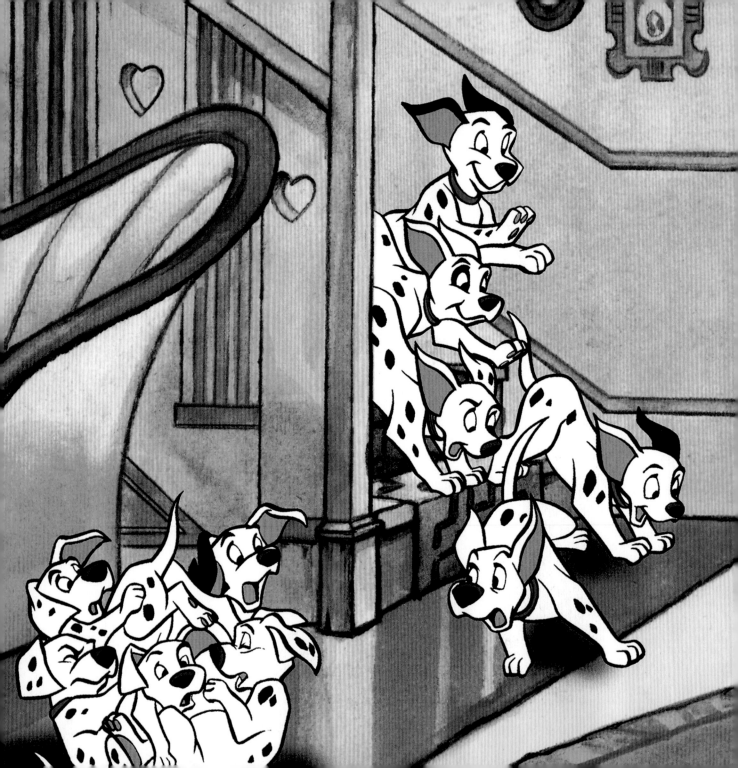

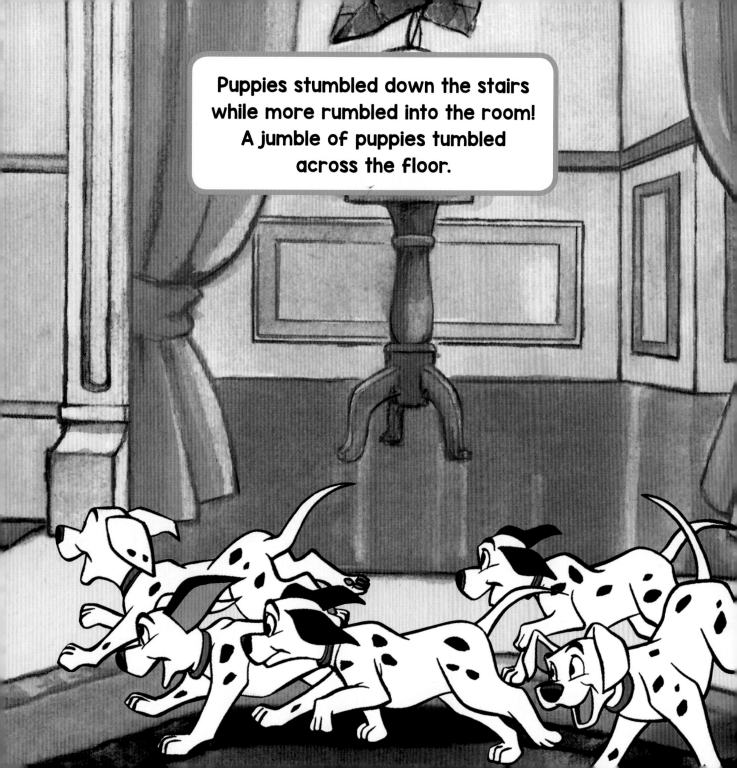

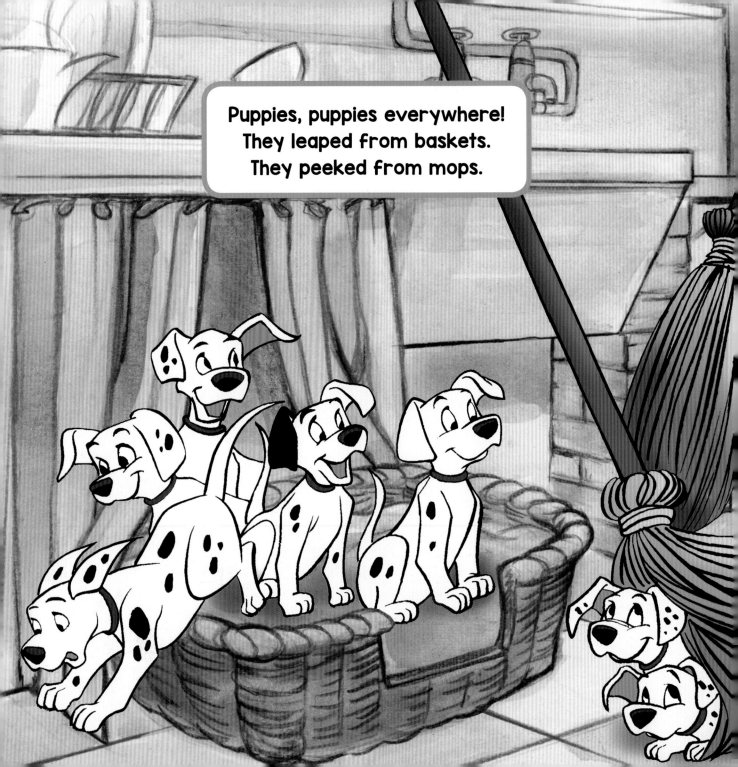

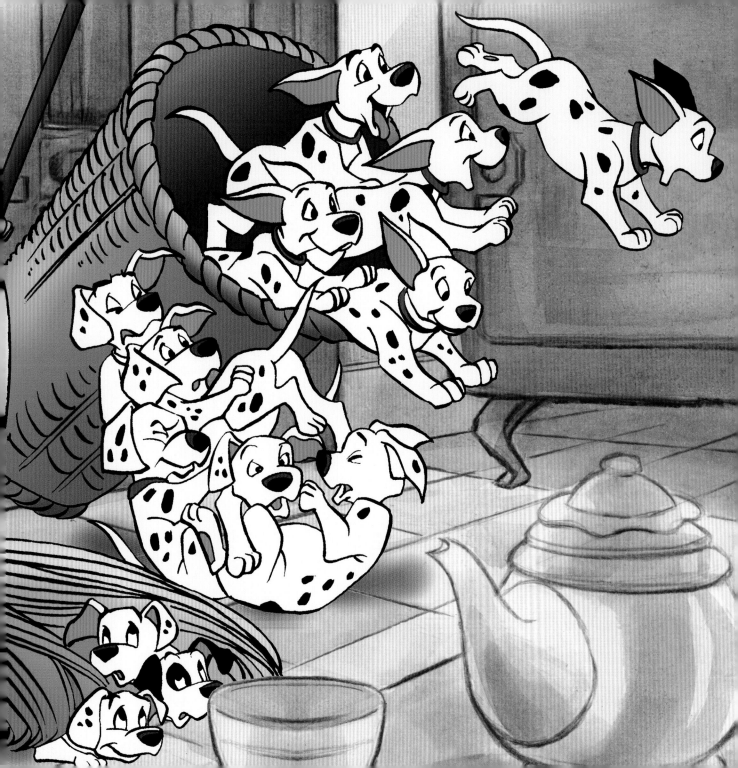

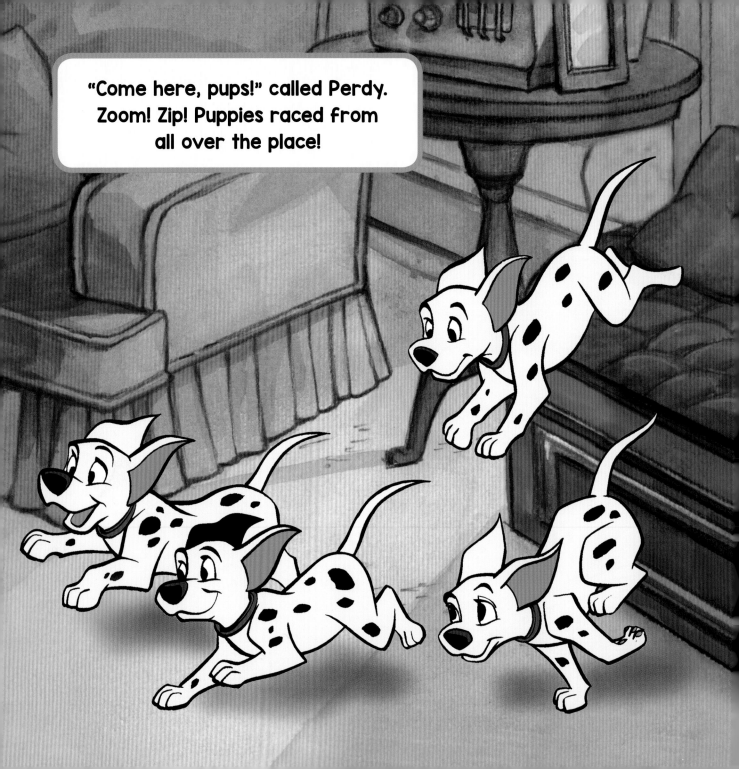

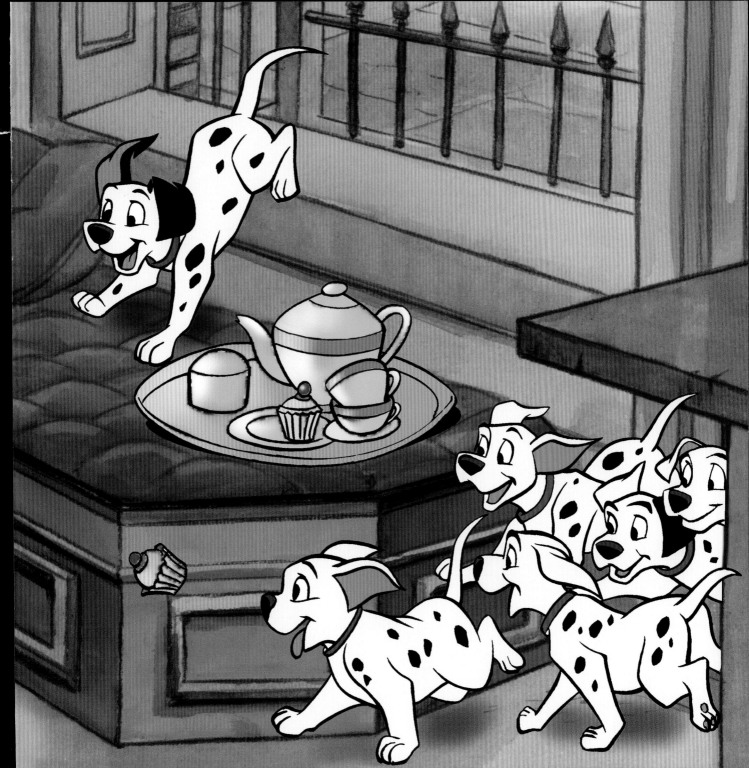

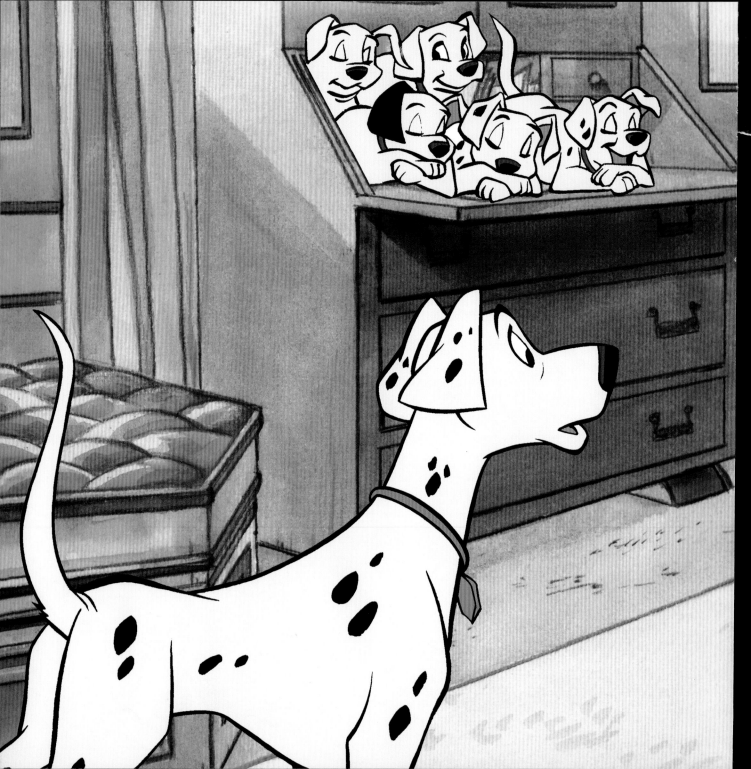

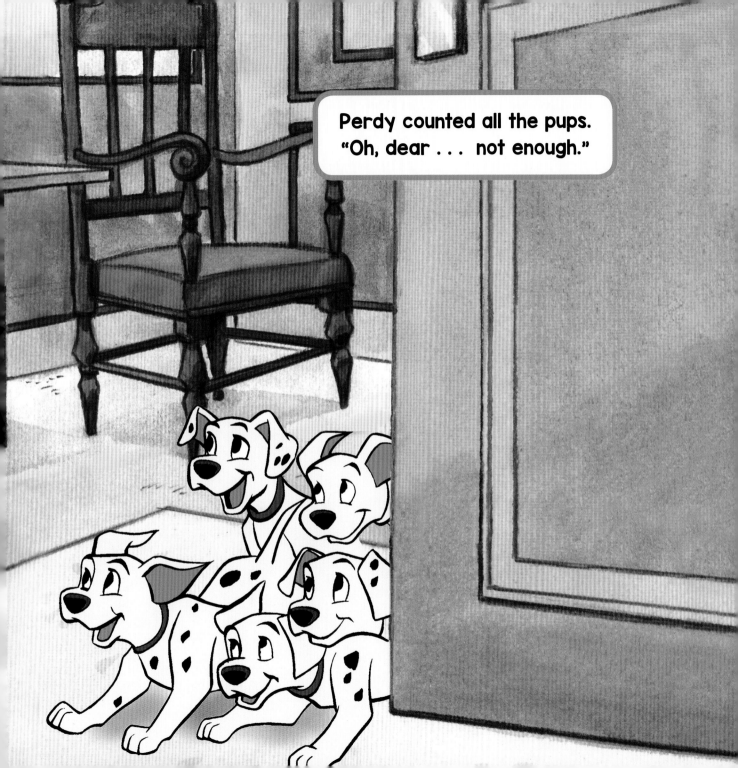

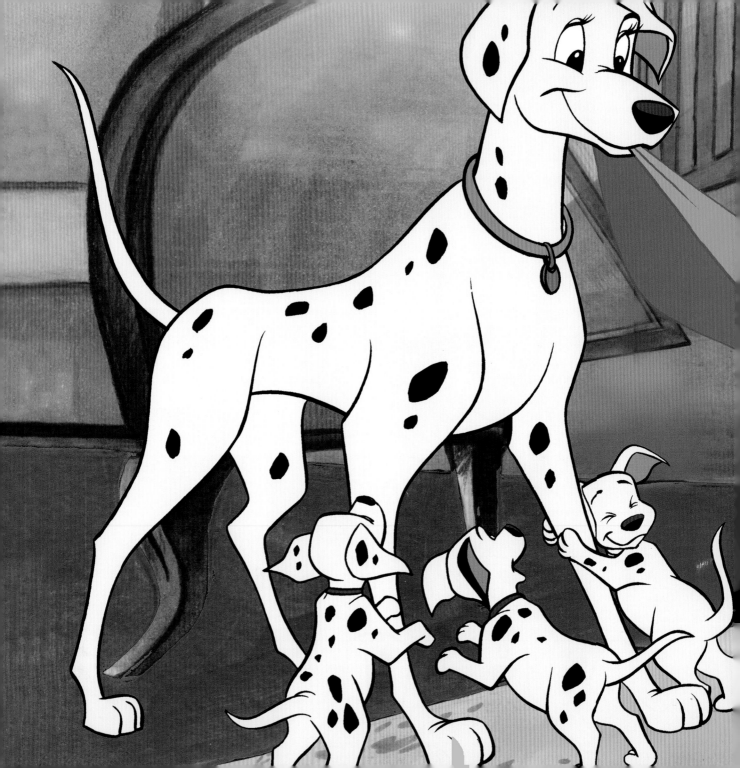

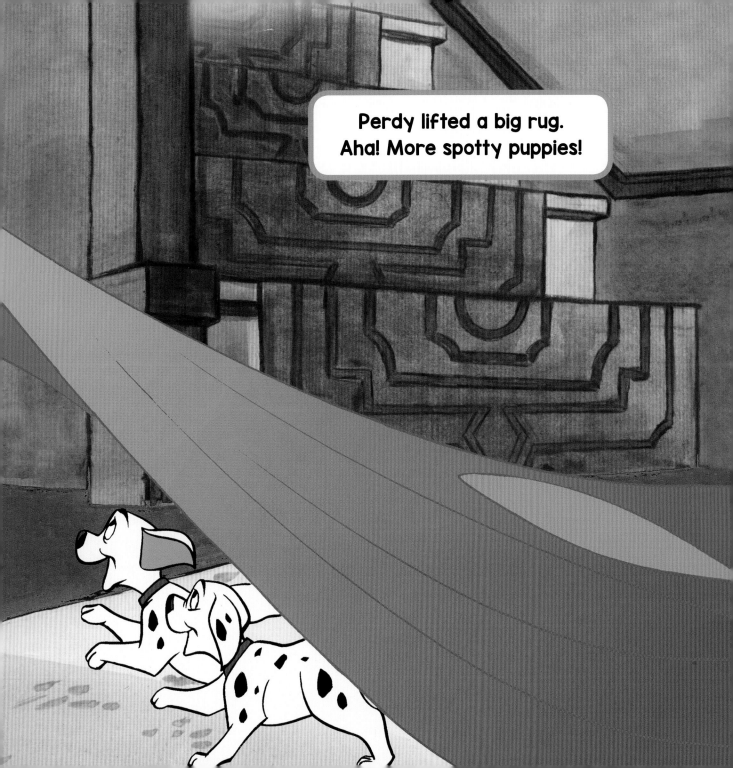

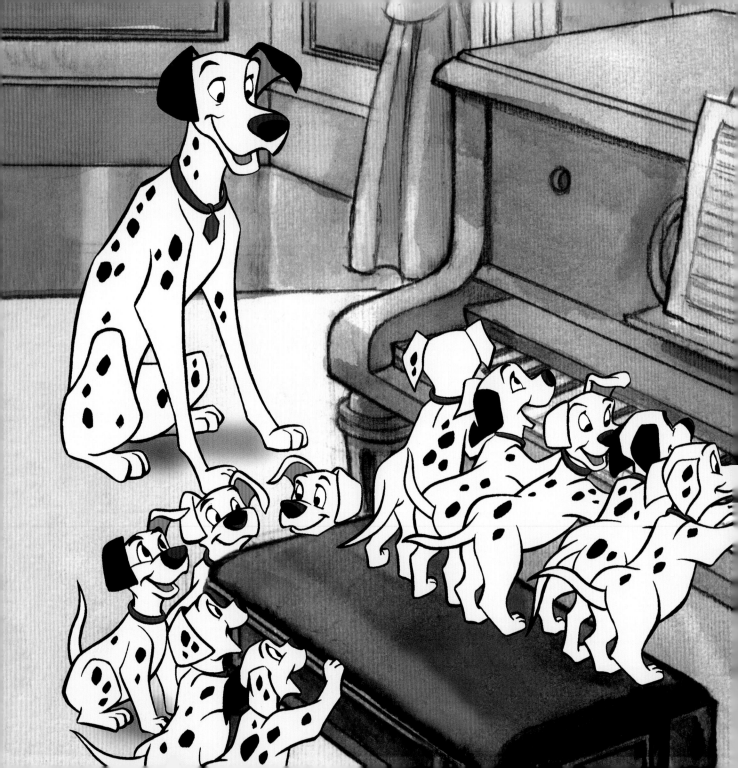

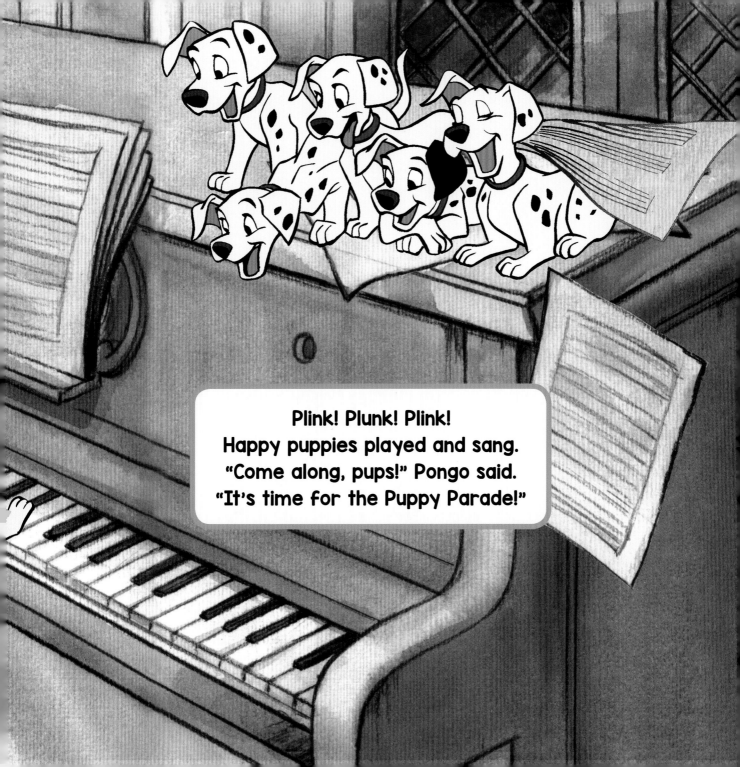

Plink! Plunk! Plink!
Happy puppies played and sang.
"Come along, pups!" Pongo said.
"It's time for the Puppy Parade!"

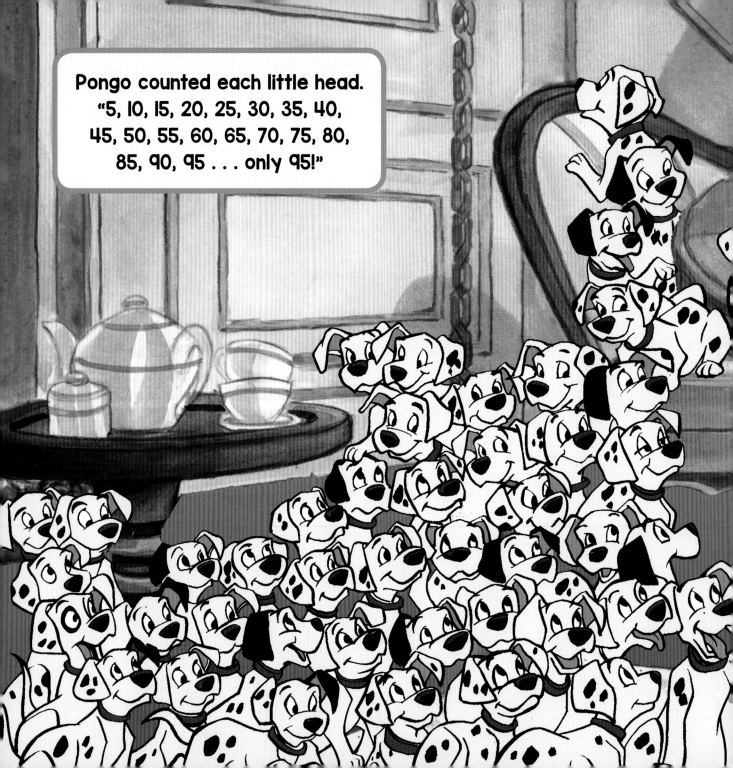

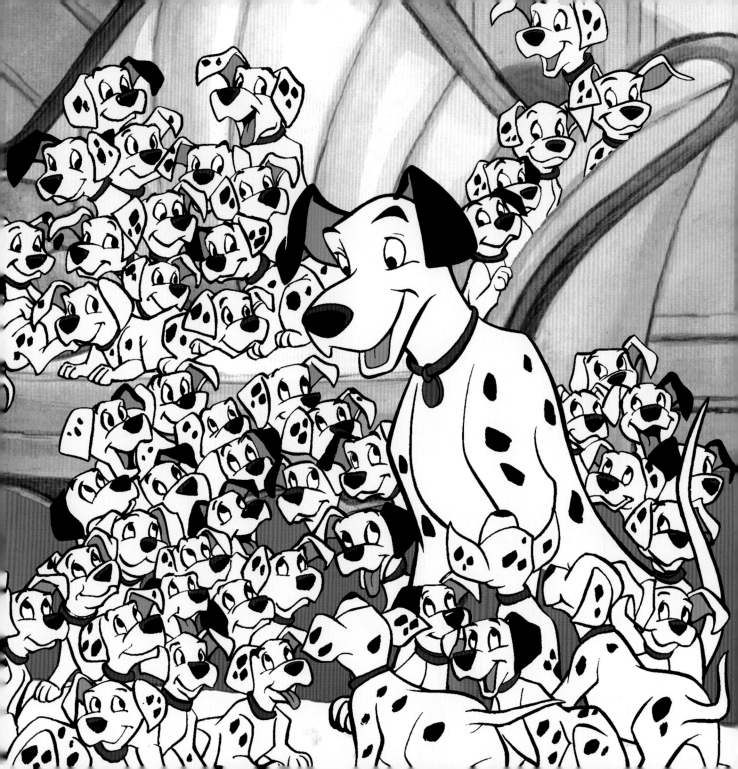

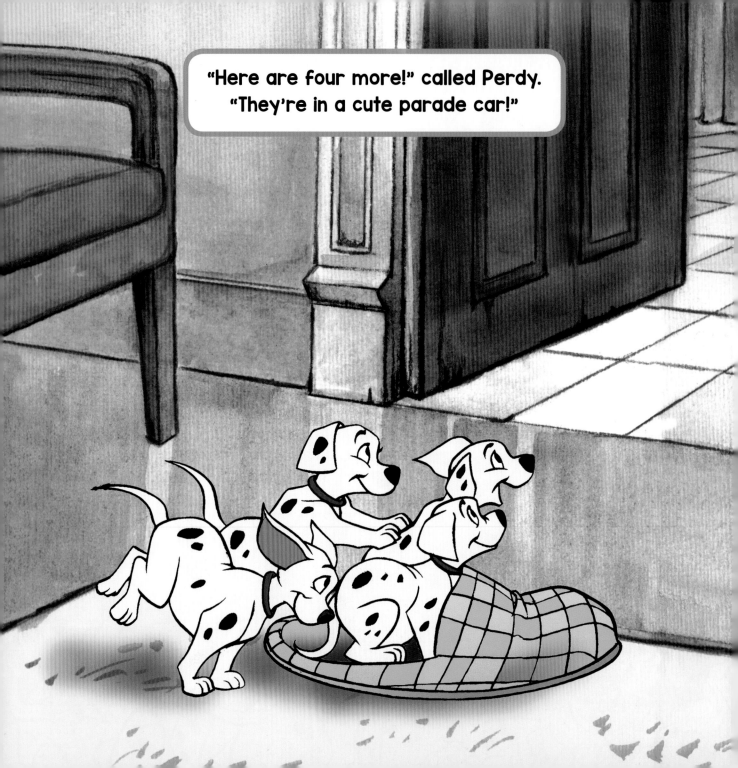

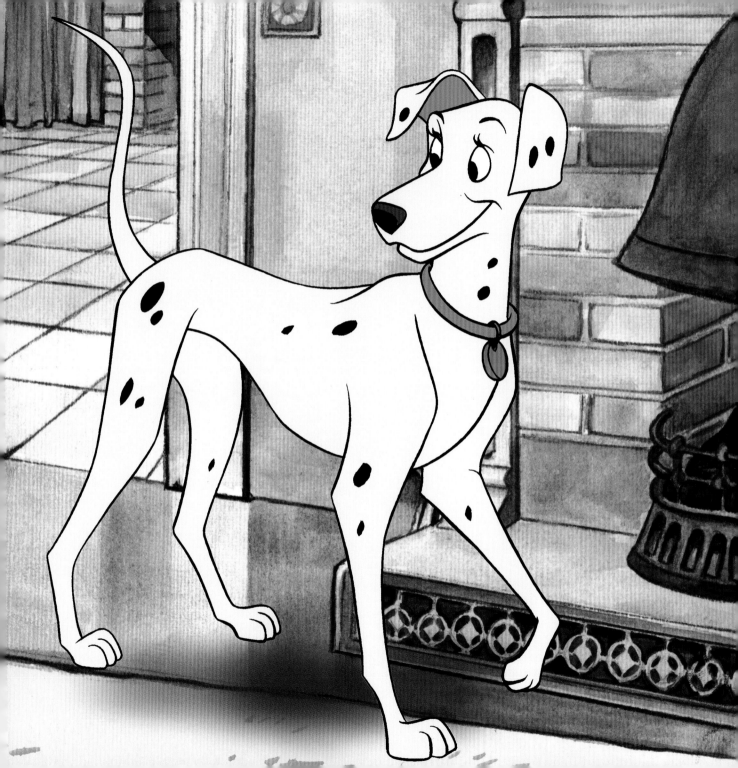

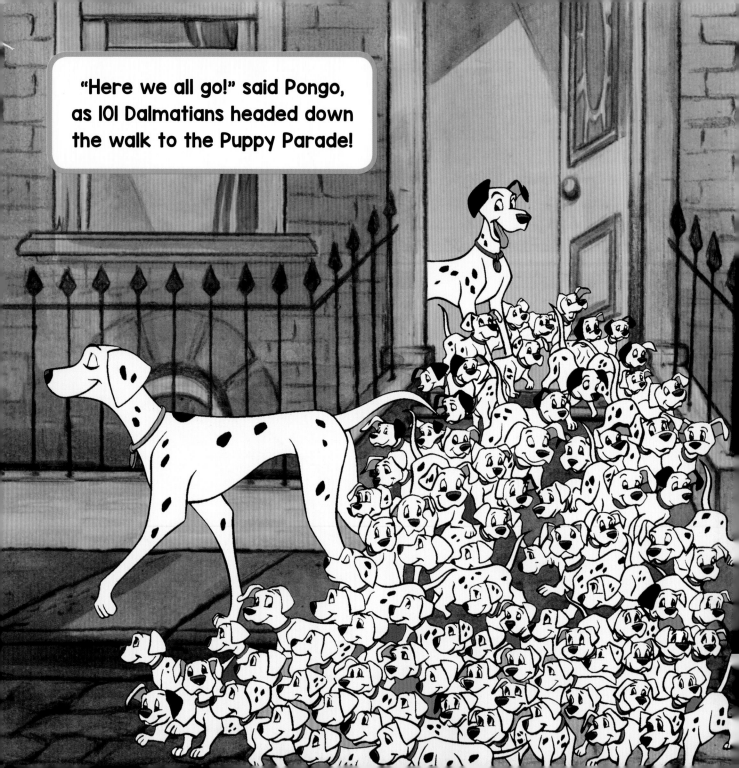